Destiny's BIG MOVE

Look for these and other books about Linelle Destiny in the Linelle Destiny Series:

Visit www.thesecretsistersclub.com

Destiny's
BIG MOVE

Dr. Alicia Holland

Illustrations by Anoop PC

This book may be ordered through booksellers or by contacting:

iGlobal Educational Services, LLC
13785 Highway 183, Suite 125
Austin, Texas 78750
www.iglobaleducation.com
512-761-5898

Because of the dynamic nature of the Internet, any web addresses or links contained in this book may have changed since publication and may no longer be valid. The views expressed in this work are solely those of the author and do not necessarily reflect the views of the publisher, and the publisher hereby disclaims any responsibility for them.

This is a work of fiction. Names, characters, businesses, places, events, and incidents are either the products of the author's imagination or used in a fictitious manner. Any resemblance to actual persons, living or dead, or actual events is purely coincidental.

Linelle Destiny Series: Destiny's Big Move

ISBN-13: 978-1-944346-13-3

Acknowledgements

I want to first honor God for placing in my heart to share my story with others. It was He whom brought Karen and I together to manifest this project. I am so grateful for Karen Hendry as she took my notes and helped write this fictitious book. There are truly no words to express my gratitude as you are truly a blessing.

I also want to thank Surendra Gupta for his creativity in formatting and Anoop PC for his creativity in bringing life to the designs and illustrations in this book series. Both of you are amazing!

Dedication

I dedicate this book series to my beautiful and talented daughters, Georgia and Amaiya Johnson. Remember, you are valued, loved, and competent. You are worthy!

Part 1
Breaking Ties

Chapter 1
Memories

Destiny is cleaning up from her lunch. It's a warm Sunday afternoon in June. She can hear the neighborhood kids playing in the street outside, the birds singing. A lawn mower is going down the street somewhere, clipping the grass nice and short, producing that luscious smell of a freshly mown lawn. Oh to be out there, Destiny thinks, tempted to go out for a walk to the ice cream parlor, but there is just too much to do.

Destiny just came back from two days in Austin, Texas. Anderson went with her and she did all of the nitty gritty required when someone moves to a new state. She found an apartment, set up her new cell phone service and utilities, and filled out all the additional paperwork for her new job. Now that she's home, she really just wants to relax for a bit, just one afternoon, but she knows time is tight. She moves in five weeks!

Destiny is just washing up the last of her lunch dishes when Momma comes into the kitchen.

"How was your trip?" asks Momma. Destiny got in late last night and slept through church that morning, so she hadn't seen Momma yet.

"It was fine, Momma," says Destiny, drying her hands. "I found the nicest little apartment, one bedroom and a cute little kitchen."

"Does it get lots of light?" asks Momma. "The last thing you want is to live in some dark little cave with no light."

"Yes, Momma. I have windows that face south for lots of sunlight. My plants will be very happy and so will I."

"Well, that's good. You need to be happy enough for both of use, sugar, because you was only gone two days and I was going crazy missing ya."

"Oh, Momma," Destiny gives her Momma a hug. "I know it, but you'll get used to it. And you know I'll come and visit. It's not that far away! Just think if I was going to New York or Chicago or somewhere like that."

"I would prefer down the street," says Momma, "but I guess Texas ain't so bad. Have you started packing, yet?"

"No," answers Destiny.

"Well, child, you better get going. You know you don't want to leave it to the last minute."

"I know, Momma. I was just telling myself I have too much to do to go outside and enjoy this beautiful day."

"Good," says Momma. "Well, off with ya! Your things won't pack themselves."

"I need to go get some boxes first," says Destiny.

Momma shoes her out of the kitchen. "Your Pop has some set aside down at the store. Go on then and get 'em."

✧ ✧ ✧

Destiny is picking up her keys by the front door when she notices a letter addressed to her. It's from Alvin! Putting her keys back down, Destiny takes the letter to her room and sits on her bed. She feels so excited as she opens the letter. She hasn't heard from Alvin in a while.

Destiny reads the letter, getting more excited with every line.

Dear Destiny,

I hope you are doing great with your studies and your teaching. I am fabulous! My track team will be competing in Austin, Texas this summer, which will bring me a little closer to you. I wish I was going to Louisiana because then we might be able to see each other. Maybe it will happen another time. Stay well.

Alvin

Alvin will be competing in Austin this summer! Destiny realizes he has no idea she's moving there. Won't that be a wonderful surprise for him?

Destiny gets out some paper and a pen and writes a quick letter back to Alvin, letting him know she will be moving to Austin and can see him when he's there. She addresses and stamps the envelope and takes the letter with her. On her way out the door, letter in hand, Momma calls out, "You ain't gone yet, child?"

"No just leaving," replies Destiny. "You need anything at the store?"

"No, sugar, I'm fine."

Destiny drives to the grocery store. It's a short drive, just ten minutes, but she has her windows down to feel the warm air. The birds are singing and she just breathes it all in.

She parks by the store, gets out, and walks down the block to mail her letter. She is thrilled as she drops it in the mailbox. Then she heads to the grocery store. It takes Destiny no time at all to find Pop.

"Hi, Pop. Momma said you have some boxes set aside for me?"

"Sure do, honey." Pop turns to one of the guys working on the floor. "Jimmy, will you please go and get the stack of boxes just inside the store room? Destiny is taking them home to pack her things."

"Yes, sir," says Jimmy and off he goes.

"I don't think I know him," says Destiny after Jimmy is gone.

"I reckon you don't know anyone in here now, save myself and a couple of the other managers. People come and people go."

"I guess," says Destiny. "It's just so strange."

Jimmy comes back with the boxes. Destiny gives Pop a kiss on the cheek and leads Jimmy out to her car, opening the trunk so he can put the boxes in.

"Thanks," says Destiny.

"No problem," says Jimmy. "You know, your Pop's super."

"Yeah I know it." Destiny gets in her car and drives home.

At home, Destiny lugs the boxes to her room. Boxes are heavier than she thought. She has some packing tape, so she tapes a couple of boxes open so she can start putting things into them. Then she opens her closet.

As she starts pulling things out of her closet, Destiny finds her old journals, the ones she used to keep in middle and high school. She opens one of them and on the first page there it is in big bold letters:

SECRET SISTERS CLUB

Tears begin to well in Destiny's eyes and roll silently down her cheeks. She sniffs and wipes her face with the back of her hand. Why on earth am I crying, she wonders.

Common sense prevails and Destiny knows it's just an emotional time for her. Seeing all these old memories, thinking about her old friends and about the things that are done and gone, along with the move she is about to make, leaving home for the first time. Fresh tears well up and Destiny lets them spill out.

But there are new memories to be made, thinks Destiny as she places her journals into one of the boxes. Besides, once she moves and get settled in her new teaching job, Destiny plans to start the Secret Sisters Club back up, bringing in new girls that can help make the world a better place.

There is so much to do, thinks Destiny. She blows her nose and gets busy with her packing, her thoughts straying to the new Secret Sisters Club and to Alvin. She can't wait to see him!

Chapter 2
Giving Notice

Yesterday, Destiny was feeling so good because she had accomplished a lot of packing, but that feeling has gone away because today she is giving her two-week notice for leaving her job at the jewelry store.

Destiny has very much enjoyed working at the jewelry store and she wants to leave on good terms in case she ever needs a job with them again. Although her future seems to be taking a different direction, it's always best not to close doors behind you. Never say never, as Momma always says.

When Destiny gets to work, her boss, Mr. Milestone, is busy with a customer. He nods to her before she puts her purse in the backroom. When she comes out, that customer is gone, but the store is filled with other customers and both Destiny and Mr. Milestone are too busy for her to speak with him. The next thing Destiny knows, it's break time and her morning is completely gone.

Destiny walks through the mall, on her way to the food court to get something to eat. Even though she doesn't feel very hungry, she knows she needs to eat something. She picks up a sub and starts to head to a table when she sees Anderson. She waves to him to come over and sits down.

"Is this seat taken?" he asks in a mock gentlemanly manner.

"Hi, Anderson," says Destiny. "Just sit down."

"Okay, what's up?" Anderson asks as he sits down across from Destiny, his dark eyes questioning her more than his words.

"I have to give my notice at the store today and I'm nervous."

"What are you nervous about?"

Destiny sighs. "I don't know. That Mr. Milestone will be angry or disappointed."

"Destiny, people quit their jobs all the time. It's really not a big deal."

"I guess," says Destiny. "What about you? You've worked at the music store for a long time. Will you be nervous when you give your notice?"

Anderson shrugs. "I haven't really thought about it much."

"What do you mean? You're going to have to give your notice soon. You're moving to Austin a month after me."

"Yeah, I know," says Anderson. "I'll get around to it. I just have a lot going on right now, planning things out. Getting ready for what the future holds," he finishes in a grand voice, with a flourish of his hands.

"Sure," says Destiny. She wraps up her barely-eaten sub and stands up. "I have to get back now. Wish me luck."

"Good luck," says Anderson, kissing Destiny on the cheek. Then he's off to the music store and Destiny is left to walk back to work, fretting in her mind about what to say.

When destiny gets back to the Jewelry store things are quiet. Not one customer is there. "Has it been quiet the whole time I was gone?" asks Destiny.

"Not quite this quiet, but not too busy either," says Mr. Milestone, straightening his blue and white tie. "Although, I think this is the first break from customers I've had all day."

"A break is a good thing," says Destiny, not sure how to start. She has put her sub in the back room and now she's fidgeting with the latch on one of the jewelry cases.

"Is something on your mind, Destiny?" asks Mr. Milestone. He walks over to where Destiny is standing. "You seem distracted today."

"Mr. Milestone, I'll be leaving the store," Destiny blurts out.

"Leaving?"

"I mean leaving my job, here at the jewelry store."

"I see," says Mr. Milestone.

"You see, I have been looking for a full-time teaching job, but with the hiring freeze here in Louisiana there just aren't any. So I got a job in Austin, Texas and I'll be moving there in a few weeks."

Destiny waits in the brief silence after she is done speaking. Then, Mr. Milestone gives her a big hug. "Destiny, that's wonderful! Congratulations!"

"You're not upset or anything?"

"About what?" asks Mr. Milestone. "About you leaving? I think it's about time you moved on in your career and found a good teaching job. I'll miss you around here, don't get me wrong, but this is so great for you."

"Thank you, Mr. Milestone!" Destiny doesn't know what else to say. A customer comes into the store and starts browsing the engagement rings.

"Of course, you'll always have a job here with us if you need one, Destiny," says Mr. Milestone, "but I really don't think that will ever be necessary."

"Thank you."

"You will come and visit whenever you're in town?"

"I sure will!" says Destiny.

"I think that customer requires some help." Mr. Milestone is pointing at the customer Destiny noticed. He winks at her.

"Yes, sir. And thanks again."

Relief floods through Destiny as she makes her way over the engagement rings. "Hello, sir," she greets the customer. "Is there anything I can help you with?"

Life is very, very good!

Chapter 3
Tutoring

Destiny thought that giving her notice at the jewelry store would be the tough part, but the evening after she spoke with Mr. Milestone she is leaving her very last tutoring session and has to say goodbye to her student, Rowena. She is packing up her things after the tutoring session is over and Rowena comes over to her and gives her a big hug.

Destiny hugs Rowena back and sees Rowena's mother, Teresa, watching. "She's gonna miss you, you know," says Teresa.

Rowena steps back and looks at Destiny, nodding her head full of curls. "I really am. I don't know how I'll get through math without you."

"Oh, honey," Destiny says, "you'll do just fine. You know more than you think and you have learned how to reason and follow the right methods. You've learned the language of math. That's all you need."

"I'll still miss you," says Rowena.

"We all will," says Teresa.

"I'll miss all of you, too." Destiny picks up her bag. "Well, goodbye."

"Good luck with your move and your new job," says Teresa. "Please, let us know how you're making out once you get settled."

"I sure will." With her bag slung over her shoulder, Destiny opens the door and steps out onto the front steps of the house. She looks back and Rowena smiles at her. Destiny waves and Rowena waves back and then Rowena shuts the door as Destiny walks down the steps to her car.

When Destiny gets in her car, she just sits there for a moment. This is it. This is the last time she will ever tutor a student in Many, Louisiana, her home town. It's probably the last time she will ever tutor anyone in Louisiana.

The tears come and Destiny lets them. It's okay to get emotional when it comes to leaving her kids behind. She has seen these kids grow from shy, nervous math kids into confident kids who have blown their teachers away with the improvements they have made.

But along with these thoughts, Destiny also realizes that if she wants to keep helping kids, then she is going to have to get her tutoring business started in Texas. There is no time like the present to place an advertisement in the Austin newspaper so she can start lining up new clients.

When Destiny walks through the door at home, she can hear voices in the kitchen. Then Momma calls out, "Is that you, Destiny?"

"Yes, Momma." Destiny puts her keys on the stand by the door and hangs her bag on a hook and then goes into the kitchen. Michelle is sitting at the table and Momma is making Destiny a cup of tea. Destiny sits at the table across from Michelle and Momma places a steaming mug in front of her. Then Momma takes off her flowered apron and hangs it on a hook by the stove and sits down.

"Thanks," Destiny says.

"Well, how did it go?" asks Michelle.

"It went fine," Destiny answers, "but it's hard to say goodbye."

"That's true enough," says Momma. "Goodbyes are always hard."

"I'm not sure which was harder," says Destiny. "Giving my notice to Mr. Milestone or saying goodbye to Rowena and her family. At least I'll see Mr. Milestone again a couple more times. Plus, he was so wonderful and happy for me. But leaving my kids, the ones I've been working with for so long, that's really tough."

"Will you keep tutoring when you go to Austin?" asks Michelle, taking a sip of her tea.

My tea is still too hot to drink so I blow on it as I nod. Momma put my tea in my favorite yellow mug and I smile as I look at it. "I was just thinking about that and I am going to write up an ad for the Austin newspaper. If I put the ad out now, then I'll be able to start getting new students in place for when I get there."

"Well, that sounds like a good plan, sugar," says Momma.

"I just hope I get new students. Austin is much bigger than Many and there are probably already loads of tutors there."

"That might be true, but there aren't any tutors there like you," says Momma.

"What do you mean?" Destiny asks.

"Honey, you got a way about you. You always have. You got the ability to get people movin', to get them excited and see what you want them to see. You'll be just fine, child. You'll see."

Michelle nods. "She's right, squirt. You have an effect on people. You just attract them. You'll have more students than you know what to do with before long."

Destiny sips her tea, which is a little cooler now. "I hope you're right," she says.

"We are," says Michelle.

Then the topic of conversation turns to Michelle's kids and what's happening in the neighborhood. Destiny sips her tea and enjoys the company of her Momma and sister. She will miss these times.

After she's finished her tea and says goodbye to Michelle and goodnight to Momma and Pop, Destiny goes into her bedroom and gets out a piece of paper and a pen. Then she thinks about her ad for the Austin paper and begins to write. It takes her a few minutes to get the words right, but then she reads it.

Does Your Child Need Help with Math?

Don't know where to turn?

GET YOUR MIND RIGHT TUTORING

6 years' experience!

Every child has the ability to learn math.

Don't give up! Believe!

Destiny adds her cell phone number to the ad and sets it on her desk. She will call the paper in the morning and have the ad run in the Saturday paper for the next four weeks.

With her tutoring business taken care of and her notice given at the jewelry store, Destiny realizes she is letting go of the last of her life in Louisiana. Something that always seemed so far off in the future is suddenly very real and Destiny feels a sensation of panic. Her heart begins to pound and tears begin to flow for the second time that day.

Maybe she is wrong to move to Austin. After all, everything she knows is here, in Louisiana. But she knows, even with all the emotion surging through her, that this is the right move. There just isn't anywhere left to grow and move in Louisiana, not right now. Her only real option is to move away and she has a sure thing set up in Austin.

"Linelle Destiny Sycamores," Destiny says to herself. "You will go to Austin and you will be just fine there. You'll see."

Not entirely convinced by her voice of reason, Destiny dresses for bed and turns out the light. She needs a good night's sleep because has so much to do before moving day. Despite this, it takes a long time to fall asleep.

Part 2
Preparations

Chapter 4
Anderson

"**M**omma!" Destiny calls as she comes out of her room and heads for the front door. "Momma?"

Momma comes out of the kitchen. "What's all the yellin' for, child?"

"Sorry, Momma. I just wanted to let you know I'm going out and won't be here for dinner."

"Anderson?" asks Momma.

Destiny nods. "He's meeting me at the diner."

"Okay, well have fun, sugar," says Momma as she gives Destiny a kiss on the cheek.

"I will, Momma. I shouldn't be home too late."

Destiny goes out the door and gets into her car. She is excited to make plans with Anderson for when they are both living in Austin.

The diner is busy when Destiny arrives. She looks for Anderson and she sees him. He managed to get their favorite booth, the one next to the window at the back of the diner. It's away from the door so it is quieter and less drafty. Destiny walks over and Anderson stands up and gives her a hug before they sit down.

The waitress comes over after a couple of minutes. She's new. Destiny doesn't know her, but her name is Kim. "Can I take your order?" she asks.

"I ordered already," says Anderson.

"Oh, okay," I said, looking at the menu. "I'll get the cheese-burger and fries and an ice tea."

Kim writes down Destiny's order and takes the menu Destiny hands to her. "I'll bring both orders together," she says.

Once Kim is gone from the table, Anderson says, "So, how did it go the other day, when you gave your notice at work?"

Destiny realizes she hasn't even spoken to Anderson since that day in the mall, except to arrange to meet for dinner. "It went totally fine," she says, as Kim comes back with Destiny's ice tea. "Mr. Milestone was happy for me."

"Of course he was. Why wouldn't he be?"

"I don't know. No reason, I guess. I was just worried he'd be disappointed. It all worked out just fine, though. But that wasn't the hardest part. The hardest part was saying goodbye to my students."

"Yeah, I get that," says Anderson.

Kim the waitress shows up with their food and sets it on the table. "Do you need anything else," she asks.

I shake my head and Anderson says, "No, we're good, thanks."

"Anyway," says Destiny, "I'm almost ready for the move and my family is going to help me on moving day, so it's all good. What about you?"

"Me?"

"Yes, you. Have you started getting yourself organized for your move? Do you even know when that will be?"

Anderson just stares at Destiny for a moment before speaking. "Um... Well, it won't be," he says.

"What do you mean, 'it won't be?'"

"I'm not moving, Destiny."

"What? Why?"

Anderson shrugs his shoulders. "I'm just not ready, yet." When Destiny looks shocked and crestfallen, Anderson continues. "Listen, I know I said I'd move there, too, but I've been doing a lot of thinking and it's just not the right time for me. I've got my music here and things are going really well."

"But we had a deal. You were going to move there, too, and we would be starting out in a new place together. How on earth will we still be able to see each other if I'm there and you're here?"

"I don't know."

They eat in silence for a while, but Destiny doesn't really feel hungry anymore. She feels frustrated and let down. How could Anderson do this to her?

"Listen," says Anderson. "I'm still gonna support you and I'm still gonna help you move. We can find a way to make this work."

Destiny nods her head, but doesn't say anything.

"Please, Destiny," says Anderson. "Please say something. Please say you understand."

"I guess I do," Destiny finally replies. "I was just looking forward to the two of us being in Austin together."

"I know, but we'll figure it out. I really need to stay here for now."

Throughout the rest of the meal, Anderson tries his best to keep the conversation going, but Destiny doesn't say much. She tries, though. When they are done eating, Destiny says, "I really need to go. I have a lot to do."

"Are you sure," says Anderson. "I was hoping we could maybe go for a walk or something."

"No, I need to get some packing done and I'm kind of tired."

"Okay." Anderson stands up as Destiny starts taking money out of her wallet to pay for her dinner. "Oh no," says Anderson. "I've got this."

"Are you sure?"

"Yeah."

Destiny gives Anderson a hug and says goodbye and then she leaves the diner and drives home feeling very disappointed.

Destiny pulls into her driveway and turns off her car. She sits in silence for a while, the silence that fills the air after the car is turned off and everything is quiet. Destiny likes that silence because it's always so peaceful.

Her frustration with Anderson is beginning to melt away. After all, he has dreams, too. He has things he wants to accomplish in life, just as she does. And Destiny knows he feels bad for letting her down. He is still being so sweet, not just ditching her, but sticking around to offer the support she needs for her move. He could have just say see you around and never saw her again, but he didn't. There is definitely something to be said for his honor and loyalty.

As she goes into the house, she realizes she is okay with Anderson's decision. She is still disappointed, but not in him. Just that she will miss him.

"You're home early, child," says Momma. She and Pop are watching a show on T.V.

"I know," says Destiny. "I just have so much to do I didn't want to stay out late. I'm going to go pack some things."

"Okay, sugar," Mommy replies.

Destiny kisses Momma and Pop goodnight and heads to her room. After she does a little packing, she goes to bed, feeling fine with the way things are working out.

Chapter 5
Alvin's Reply

The next day is Destiny's last day at the jewelry store. The staff is all there and they give her a little going away party. Mr. Milestone is kind enough to give Destiny a beautiful necklace as a going away present. Everyone wishes Destiny good luck in Austin, although they all agree she doesn't need it because she has what it takes to succeed. Destiny hugs everyone, Mr. Milestone last, and she sees tears in his eyes.

When Destiny gets home that evening and walks in the door, she feels sad and happy all at the same time. She puts her keys on the stand by the door and notices a letter sitting there. It's addressed to her. She picks it up and looks at the return address. It's from Alvin! He wrote back!

Destiny goes into the living room and sits on the sofa. Her hands are shaking from excitement as she opens the letter. It's written in crayon! How cute is that?

Dear Destiny,

I can't believe you're moving to Austin! That is so exciting. I'm so happy for you that you have found a good, full-time teaching job now. You deserve it and you'll be great. What an exciting new adventure!

I want to see you while I'm in Austin. It will be during the last week of July. May I take you to dinner?

Circle **Yes** *or* **No**.

You can call me while I'm in Austin at 512-763-0779.

Alvin

As Destiny finishes reading Alvin's letter Momma calls out from the kitchen. "That you, Destiny?"

"Yes, Momma."

"Do you want some tea or a snack?" asks Momma.

"In a few minutes. There's something I have to do first, then I'll be in."

In her room, Destiny dances around like a schoolgirl with a crush. She is so excited that she will be able to see Alvin that she can hardly breathe. She sits down at her desk and opens his letter. Then she realizes she has no pens or markers around, they're all in boxes, and she definitely doesn't have any crayons.

Destiny runs out to the front door and grabs her purse. Back in her room, she gets out her pen and circles "Yes" on Alvin's letter. Then she writes her phone number at the bottom of the letter and signs it.

For her final touch, Destiny puts on fresh lipstick and kisses the letter beside her signature. With a big smile on her face, Destiny puts the letter in a new envelope and seals and addresses it. Then she puts a stamp on the letter and goes back out to the front door.

Destiny hangs up her purse. Then she goes outside and walks down the street. The mailbox is at the corner a few houses down, and when Destiny reaches it, she opens the mailbox door and drops the letter in. As she closes the door, she can hear the letter slide down the chute and she smiles. That sliding sound is like music to her ears.

Anderson might not be moving to Austin anymore, but now she will get to see Alvin. She has something really wonderful to look forward to when she gets to Austin, something that is connected to home. And she will get to visit with a great friend.

When Destiny goes back home, she goes straight to the kitchen, where her tea is already waiting for her. There is a plate of homemade cookies in the center of the table. Destiny sits down and watches the steam rise from the mug.

"So, squirt," says Michelle, reaching for a cookie. "You all ready to go? Moving day is coming in a couple of days."

"Almost," says Destiny, taking a sip of tea.

"I hear Anderson changed his mind about moving to Austin," says Michelle.

Destiny glances over at Momma, who winks at her. "He decided it's not the right time for him to move, but that's fine. This move is for me. It was never about him. Plus, he's been a dear about it and is still going to help on moving day."

"That's good of him," says Momma. "Shows he's got character and that he's a gentleman."

Destiny nods. Then she says, "I'm really gonna miss these tea-time conversations with you guys."

"I'm gonna miss them, too," says Michelle.

"You and Momma will still be able to have them," says Destiny.

"Yeah, but they won't be the same without you."

"They sure won't, says Momma, "but we are always just a phone call away. You can call us anytime, day or night."

"I know," Destiny replies. "But I still feel sad. It just won't be the same."

Momma reaches out her hand and places it on Destiny's hand. Momma's hand is warm and soft. Michelle places her hand on top on Momma's. "Sugar," says Momma, "you got more strength and courage than anyone I ever did know. You also got smarts. You'll be just fine, you hear? Just fine."

"She sure will," says Michelle. "I'm proud of you, squirt."

"Now, you better run along and get that packing done or you won't be ready when the time comes," says Momma. She gets up from the table and Destiny can see the tears forming in Momma's eyes, threatening to spill over and flow down her cheeks.

No, Destiny thinks, *you're the strong one, Momma, letting me go with such grace.*

But Destiny just nods and gets up from the table. "You're right," she says as she takes her tea and a couple of cookies and goes back to her room.

When she gets there, Destiny just sits on the edge of her bed for a while, sipping her tea and eating a cookie and thinking about what's to come. She didn't think this many emotions could possibly exist inside a person all at the same time.

Then a knock comes at Destiny's bedroom door and Michelle pokes her head in. "Do you need any help?" she asks.

"No," says Destiny. "I don't have much left to do. But thanks."

"Momma really is proud of you, ya know. Pop, too."

"I know."

"Okay, get to it then," says Michelle. "I'll see you tomorrow."

There are still a few things left in Destiny's closet that she needs to go through. She has a few boxes in the corner of her room that are going to be donated. The rest of it goes with her.

Destiny realizes her whole life has been put into boxes to be moved to another state. It's overwhelming, yet the giddiness inside is almost more than she can bear. She sets to work, knowing she has one last day at home before her life changes forever.

Chapter 6
Big Plans

The sound of the packing tape being pulled to seal the last box is loud in the evening silence of Destiny's bedroom. Destiny puts the tape down and picks up the box, depositing it on the pile in the corner of her room. She is finally done all of her packing, which is a good thing, considering tomorrow is moving day.

Destiny gets herself ready for bed, dressing in her favorite yellow and blue PJs, and climbs into bed. She closes her eyes and tries to settle, breathing deeply. Unfortunately, after lying in bed for several minutes, sleep doesn't come.

Destiny turns over to lie on her back, eyes open, staring up at the ceiling, even though it's too dark to see it. Her mind is just so busy with everything that is happening. She is excited about seeing Alvin in just a couple of weeks. She hasn't seen him in so long and the fact that he asked to see her means he still cares.

Destiny is also excited about the move tomorrow. She is going to sleep in her new apartment tomorrow night, all by herself, in a new city. The thought both excites and terrifies her. She has never been away from home before, not permanently anyway. Sure, she has stayed away for a summer program at a university, but that was in a residence. This is different. All her things will be with her, her belongings in a new room that is hers, but in a new place.

Destiny's family will be there to start loading the truck early in the morning, so Destiny will be up by at least 6:00 am. But no matter how early she has to get up, it doesn't make it any easier to fall asleep.

With a sigh, Destiny gets up and puts on her bathrobe. Maybe if she gets a glass of milk, she will be able to sleep. She makes her way to the kitchen.

The light is already on in the kitchen when Destiny gets there. Destiny finds Pop sitting at the table, drinking a glass of milk and eating one of Momma's cookies.

"What are you doing up, Pop?" asks Destiny.

"Couldn't sleep," he answers. "You?"

"Same," says Destiny, getting a glass out of the cupboard. "Too excited about the move tomorrow."

"Yeah," says Pop. "I'm thinkin' about the move tomorrow, too. I'm thinkin' about how I'm about to lose my baby girl." He looks up at Destiny and his face seems more lined, older than it usually does.

"Oh, Pop. You're not losing me," says Destiny. She brings her glass of milk over and sits at the table next to Pop. Then she reaches out her hand and places it on his. "I won't be that far away and I'll come home and visit. You know that."

"I know, honey. This move is good for you, I know that. You have the chance to get out of this small town and make something of yourself. You got the smarts and you need to use them. I'm just gonna miss ya, is all."

"I'm gonna miss you, too, Pop. And Momma and Michelle and everyone." Destiny can feel a lump forming in her throat. She takes a sip of milk, as though she might be able to swallow the lump with the milk and make it go away. It doesn't work.

"Well, I'm mighty proud of ya, Destiny. You've done us all proud." Destiny is sure she can see the glistening of tears in Pop's eyes.

"Thanks, Pop." She can fill her own eyes begin to fill up, accompanying the pesky lump that is still sitting in her throat.

"Well, better at least try to get some sleep tonight," says Pop, brusquely. Pushing his chair back and getting up. He goes over and kisses the top of Destiny's head, letting his hand linger on her shoulder for a moment. Then he says, "Goodnight, sweetie," and he's gone.

Back in her room, her glass of milk dutifully drank in the hopes of finding sleep soon, Destiny is still too wired to settle down. She pulls out her journal, which she decided she wouldn't pack away in a box, and opens it up to a blank page. She might as well start making plans for her tutoring business and the Secret Sisters Club.

Now that she will be going to teach at a school permanently and she will have a class of her own, Destiny can start her Secret

Sisters Club once again. She can share the beauty of it with the girls at her new school and help them learn the skills of leadership, cooperation, and personal development.

This time, the club will be targeted to girls in middle school. This means that Destiny will have to consider what types of activities, events, and projects she will need to come up with to challenge them.

Destiny considers this carefully. The girls can hold elections, the same way Destiny and her friends did when she first started the club. The girls can also be part of a conversation about the direction the club should go in. They can also hold a fundraiser of some sort to help raise money for the club. There are so many possibilities! Destiny writes down the ones that come to mind:

- ♥ *Move to a weekend model to mentor girls*
- ♥ *Bring Alvin onboard to help mentor boys*

Destiny definitely wants to reach out to boys, too. After she writes down her ideas for the Secret Sisters Club, she turns her thoughts to her tutoring business. Get Your Mind Right Tutoring has been such a success in Many, Louisiana, but what about a big city like Austin?

Destiny did advertise in the Austin newspaper, but so far she has only had two phone calls. She also sent out an email to all of her current clients, offering to tutor them online. But Destiny has had some ideas of what she wants to do to expand her tutoring business. She writes her ideas down in her journal so she doesn't have to worry about forgetting any of them.

- ◎ *Write a book on How to Start a Home-Based Tutoring Business*
- ◎ *How to Hire Help for the Tutoring Business*

When she is done writing, Destiny looks at the list. They are good ideas that she is sure she will use in the future, especially as she grows her business. That's one benefit of Austin being a big city. If she can get the word out and there is a need for tutoring, then there is a huge population of students from which she can get new clients.

With all the ideas out of her head and on paper, Destiny just stares at her journal for a few minutes, not really focusing on it, but instead thinking about the move tomorrow. She can't get it out of her mind!

However, she is beginning to feel at least a little sleepy. Destiny tucks her journal away in her suitcase and gets into bed. She lays there and looks around her room for a while, thinking about all the years that this was her bedroom. She can remember when she was just a little girl in this room, with all her toys. She used to love reading books and playing with her Barbie dolls. The memories feel so fresh in a way, even though a lot of them are very old.

Then Destiny turns out her light and closes her eyes. Despite the feeling of being tired, it still takes her a long time to fall asleep. When she finally does, she dreams that Alvin is driving her moving truck and she is sitting beside him. It's a pleasant dream.

Part 3
Moving Day

Chapter 7
Family Help

Destiny is awake before the sun is up. She lays in bed for a while, watching as the very first rays of sunlight illuminate the curtains in her window, making them glow a soft blue in the fading darkness. She can hear someone up and about. Probably Momma putting the coffee on.

Destiny gets out of bed and goes to have a quick shower. Then she gets dressed for the day, putting on some comfortable sweats, good traveling clothes, as Momma says. When she is ready, she packs the last of her things, her toiletries and PJs, in her suitcase and sets the suitcase beside the bedroom door.

By the time Destiny gets to the kitchen, the sun is up and shining through the kitchen window. "Morning, Momma," Destiny says as she pours herself a cup of coffee and sits at the table.

"Mornin', sugar," replies Momma. "How'd ya sleep?"

"Not that great, but I don't feel tired."

"That's just cause you're excited," says Momma. "You might not sleep well tonight either, but tomorrow night you'll sleep like the dead."

Destiny can hear Pop getting up. Then she hears the sound of a big truck outside, the motor cutting through the early morning silence like a chainsaw revving up in the quiet of the forest.

"There's your brother and Demarcus," says Momma.

A couple of minutes later Destiny hears the front door open and shortly Dino comes into the kitchen. "Hello there, Momma," he says, going over and planting a kiss on her cheek. Momma slaps his arm and then goes to pour him a coffee.

"Hey, sis. Ready?"

"Morning, Dino," says Destiny. "As ready as I'll ever be."

"I'll grab some coffee and then me and Demarcus will get loading the stuff stored in the garage." He turns and Momma hands him a mug. "Momma, you just know what I want."

"Uncle Walter and the boys should be here soon, too," says Momma. Destiny's nephews Alexander and Carlos and her Uncle Walter are helping load the truck. Destiny's Pop can't help load because of his bad back, but he is sure to be directing everyone.

Destiny has always been good at saving money and it has paid off because she has been able to purchase everything she needs, except a dining table. She will look for a table when she gets to Austin. The furniture is stored in the garage and the men are loading all of that before they come in and get her boxes. Destiny is grateful for their help.

An hour later, the truck is loaded. During that time, Momma, Michelle, and Destiny have been in the kitchen cooking up a big breakfast. They told Destiny she wasn't to lift a finger, but she insisted. "I can't just sit here and do nothing. I'll go crazy!" In the end, Destiny mixed the pancake batter.

With the loading done, the whole family gathered in the kitchen, filling their plates full of good food that would keep them fueled for much of the day. Some people sit at the kitchen table; others go into the living room or on the front step to eat their food.

Breakfast is so good and Destiny fills up with a second plate of pancakes and bacon. When she is done, Destiny is certain her stomach will burst. "I'll miss your cooking, Momma," Destiny says as she takes her plate to the sink.

"I know you will, sugar," says Momma with a big grin on her face. "It doesn't matter who you are or how old you get, you always gonna miss your Momma's cookin'. Now go on into the living room."

Momma walks behind Destiny and shouts out to everyone, "After everyone brings their dishes to the kitchen, gather in the living room, please."

There is commotion for a while as everyone cleans up their dishes. It's at this time that Anderson arrives. He couldn't make it in time to help load, but he will be there to help unload at the other end.

"Looks like I missed a good breakfast," he says.

Destiny nods, but before she can say anything, Pop speaks up. "Now, everyone knows our little girl is leaving home and I know by now all of you have told her how much you will miss her. But no one will miss Destiny more than Momma and I."

Pop turns to me, Momma standing by his side holding an envelope in her hand. The tears are already streaming down Momma's face.

Pop continues, "I'll keep this short. Destiny, honey, no one else in the family has got as much education as you and no one has made such a big move or gone as far away. We will miss you, but we are also very proud of you. You have shown a lot of courage."

Momma continues, "When you get to Austin and we come home, you won't be all alone. You can call us anytime you need to, but you will also have a little extra money to help you get started."

Momma hands Destiny the envelope she is holding. Destiny opens it. Inside she finds a going away card and a $300 gift card for Hometown Franks Grocery & More. "Oh, thank you!" she says.

"Now, that's for food and clothing and whatever else you need. You use that wisely, child. And don't go calling home *all* the time. You need to budget your money the way I taught you to."

"Yes, Momma," says Destiny between the sobs that have started pouring out of her.

Destiny goes to hug Momma and Pop hugs them both. His cheeks are wet. Michelle is crying, too.

Soon, Momma is all business, again. "We need to get on the road and there is still cleaning up to do."

"I'll take care of cleaning up from breakfast," says Michelle. "Y'all just get ready to go."

A few minutes later, Destiny is standing outside the house with Momma, Pop, Michelle, and Dino. Anderson hangs back by Destiny's car. Destiny is staring at the house.

"This is goodbye," she says.

"For now," says Pop.

"Of course, I'll come back to visit, but this won't be home anymore."

Momma turns and looks at Destiny. "Now, child, let's get one thing straight. No matter where you move or how old you get, while your Pop and I are still breathing, this will be your home! And Many will always be where your family is."

Destiny realizes Momma is right. Her family, her roots, will always be in Many, Louisiana, no matter where she goes. Destiny nods and takes Momma's hand in hers. "You're right. It will always be my home."

With that Destiny turns and walks to her car. They have a long drive ahead of them.

Chapter 8
The Drive

Destiny sits and stares out the car window at the passing countryside. They have been driving for about an hour and she is enjoying the relaxation. When Anderson offered to do the driving, she accepted without hesitation because she needs some down time and this might be all she gets for the next little while.

Destiny won't have a lot of time to get settled in Austin before she has to start work. She will be helping out with the school's summer program, so she will be starting work the week after she moves. That leaves just a few days to get unpacked, get her apartment organized, and get her bearings in her new city.

As overwhelming as it is, Destiny feels relaxed. She has what she needs and she has been to Austin before, so hopefully finding her way around won't be too much of a problem. As she stares out the window, Destiny drifts off to sleep to the peaceful rocking of the car.

Destiny is sitting in a huge room. It's fancy, with nice round dinner tables spread throughout, a deep red carpet and off-white and red table cloths covering every table. The richness of the décor and the architecture boasts of a beautiful ballroom in a nice hotel, with high arched ceilings and stunning chandeliers. Destiny's teaching peers are all around her.

Destiny is dressed in a nice evening gown. She has finished a lovely meal and is sipping a drink as she listens to someone who is talking from a podium that is situated at the front of the room.

"Her work and what she has accomplished this year is truly an example and an inspiration for all of us. And so, it gives me great pleasure to give this year's Teacher of the Year Award to Linelle Destiny Sycamores, the newest grade eight teacher from CD Heights Middle School!"

Thunderous applause erupts all around Destiny and for a moment she just sits there stunned. This has only been her first year teaching in Austin. Then Destiny gets up and walks up to the podium. When she gets there she looks out at her peers who are clapping and celebrating her. It's a wondrous feeling.

She accepts the award, a lovely trophy, and thinks about what to say. She hadn't prepared anything because she had no idea this would happen. Destiny begins with, "Thank you so much! I really appreciate this award."

Destiny wakes to find herself still in the car with the land-scape passing by at a rapid pace. She blinks a little in the bright light and sits up.

"Good morning, sleepyhead," says Anderson.

"I must have dozed off," says Destiny. "I know I didn't get much sleep last night, so I guess I needed it."

"Well, you slept for about 45 minutes, so that should make you feel better."

"Where are we?" asks Destiny.

"We'll be in Crockett soon. Should make a pit stop there."

Destiny nods, not that Anderson can see her because his eyes are on the road.

"Do you mind if I put on some music? I was gonna pop in a CD, but then you fell asleep and I didn't want to disturb you."

"Sure," says Destiny, still feeling a bit sleepy.

Anderson rummages around in a small bag that is just behind his seat and pulls out a CD. He pops it into the player and soon music fills the car. Destiny doesn't know the band and hasn't heard the song before, but she likes it. Anderson is singing along to the music and drumming his thumbs on the steering wheel and Destiny lets her mind drift.

Suddenly, Destiny sees a vision of herself holding a stack of papers. She realizes it's a manuscript she is holding, the neat type-written words filling the pages. She has written a book about tutoring and it is about to be published. This is something she has desperately wanted for some time, to be able to reach out and share her experience with other teachers and schools so they can help their students excel using methods she has proven work time and time again.

Coming back to the car and the Louisiana scenery, Destiny is thrilled with the vision she just had. Writing a book about her tutoring experience would be a fantastic way to help others. She has no idea when she will find the time, but she knows she will do it. She has to. It's all part of the bigger picture for her.

Soon, they are entering Crockett and Anderson pulls into a gas station outside of town. Once Anderson pulls up to the gas tank, Destiny welcomes the chance to stretch her legs and gets out of the car.

Anderson goes to put gas in the car, the sunlight glinting off the dark skin of his muscular arms, and Destiny says, "I'm going in to pay for the gas. You want anything?"

"Yeah, sure. I'll have a Coke, please. And some Zapp's Creole Onion chips."

"Really? Momma supplies us with a bag full of homemade snacks and you want Zapp's chips?"

"What can I say? I like their Creole Onion chips."

Destiny goes inside and looks for the chips. Then she grabs a Coke and an ice tea for herself. By the time she gets to the cash register, Anderson has finished pumping the gas. She pays for everything and thanks the cashier. Then she heads back out to the car.

Anderson has pulled up to the store front and Destiny hops into the car. Anderson opens his bag of chips and then he pulls out of gas station the parking lot and they are back on the road. While there is a little more than half their drive still ahead of them, there is a whole new life ahead of Destiny. She settles in for the rest of the drive and enjoys her ice tea and some of Momma's cookies.

Chapter 9
Late Arrivals

Anderson pulls into the parking lot of Destiny's new apartment building. The building is a light-colored, three-story brick with nice big windows. No one else has arrived yet and both Destiny and Anderson get out of the car and stretch after the long drive.

"I feel like I was folded up in that car forever," says Anderson as he reaches for the blue sky, stretching out his long, lean body.

"Me too," Destiny replies, looking around. It's a quiet late Wednesday afternoon, shortly after 3:00. They made good time on the drive. "I'll go into the office and get the keys. Dino and Demarcus should be here soon."

Destiny makes her way into the office of the apartment building. There is a short, blond woman sitting a desk, glasses perched on the end of her nose. Destiny remembers her from when she first looked at the apartment.

"Hello. Jill, right?" asks Destiny.

"Yes, dear."

"I'm here to pick up the keys to my apartment. Destiny Sycamores."

Jill looks at her computer, navigating to a certain screen, then she says, "Yes, I remember you. Moving here from Louisiana to start a teaching job, right?"

Destiny nods. "Yes, that's right."

"Wonderful." Jill stands up and walks over to a cabinet set into the wall behind her. She opens it and pulls out a set of keys. She hands them to Destiny. "There you go, for apartment 304. There is a spare in case you need it."

"Thank you very much," says Destiny.

"Are you moving in now, dear?" asks Jill.

"As soon as my brother and cousin get here with the truck. They shouldn't be too long."

"Wonderful, as long as you're done by nine o'clock. We like it a little more quiet around here after that time. And besides, it will be getting dark by then."

"Yes, mam. Thanks again."

Destiny rejoins Anderson in the parking lot. He is leaning against her car.

"Got the keys," she says, dangling them in the air.

They would go inside Destiny's apartment to wait, but there isn't anything to sit on. So they open the car doors and sit in the car, waiting for the rest of her family to come along.

It's almost five o'clock when Momma and Pop arrive, with Alexander and Carlos eager to get out of Pop's truck and get moving. They pull up alongside Destiny's car and get out.

Anderson has some music playing and turns it down a little so everyone can talk.

"Where's the truck?" asks Pop.

"They aren't here yet," answers Destiny.

"What?" says Momma. "We saw them on the road when we stopped for lunch and they got ahead of us. They should have been here an hour ago."

"I don't know," says Destiny, "but we're getting pretty hungry. We've been sitting here for a couple of hours."

"Well, they know where they're going," says Momma. "Let's go get something to eat, and if they show up while we're gone, they can take a turn waitin'"

"We saw a diner on the way here," says Anderson. "It's just a few blocks back that way." He points down the street they took into town.

"I remember seein' that place," says Pop. "Can't remember the name, but a big green sign?"

"That's the one," says Anderson.

"Let's go there and get some dinner," says Pop. To Anderson he says, "You lead the way, son."

They all get in their vehicles and a few minutes later they are sitting in a large booth in the All Star Diner with menus in their hands.

Everyone orders and drinks are put on the table. Soon the food is there and Destiny digs into her bacon cheeseburger with fries. Anderson went for the spicy Texan quarter pounder.

"I hope they're there when we get back," says Destiny. "I just want to get everything moved in before it gets too late."

By the time they leave the restaurant, it's getting close to 6:30. When they get back to Destiny's apartment building, there is still no sign of the truck.

"Well, now where could they be?" says Momma. "I hope nothing bad happened."

"If they had gotten into trouble on the road, we would have seen them," says Pop. "No, they must have gone and done something else. They got friends here?"

"I don't know," says Destiny.

"Not much to be done except wait," says Momma. "Might as well get comfortable."

Pop has a pack of cards in his glove box and they manage to play cards on the hood of Destiny's car for a while. Momma chooses to sit and read her book.

By the time 8:30 rolls around Pop says, "At this point, we ain't gonna get everything unloaded before it gets dark, even if they get here now."

Everyone agrees.

"There was a hotel up the road," says Momma. "Maybe we should go book a couple of rooms for the night."

"Good idea," says Pop. "Why don't I take you and the boys there and we'll get set up. Then I'll come back and see what's happening."

Everyone agrees and once again Destiny and Anderson are waiting on their own.

"You could have gone with 'em," says Anderson. "You'd get some rest."

"Now you know I wouldn't be able to rest not knowing where Dino and Demarcus are," Destiny replies.

Pop and Momma come back close to ten o'clock and Destiny and Anderson are still waiting. "They ain't here yet?" says Pop.

"Nope," says Anderson.

"What are you doing here, Momma?" asks Destiny.

"I can't sit around that hotel room and wait. We left Alexander and Carlos there watching TV, but I need to know what happened to those boys."

"Well, they got 'til ten thirty," says Pop, "then they on their own."

It is around quarter past ten when the truck pulls in.

"Where in tarnation have you been?" exclaims Pop when Dino gets out of the truck.

Dino glances at Demarcus and says, "Sorry y'all. We got lost."

"Lost?" says Destiny, raising her eyebrows.

"What do you mean you got lost," says Pop. "Even if you did, it wouldn't take you five hours to find your way. Fess up, boys."

"We went through Houston and got messed up."

"Now, I know we saw the truck when we stopped for lunch in Crockett," says Momma. "You tellin' me you turned south and went through Houston? What kind of story is that?"

Destiny can see Momma with her hands on her hips and that expression she gets on her face when she's really angry, the one with the crease that forms in the middle of her forehead. Dino can see it, too, and he knows what it means. Better to come clean than try to keep up a lie.

"It was my fault," Demarcus confesses after a few moments. "I have some friends here in town and we stopped by. We ended up losin' track of time. I'm aweful sorry."

Everyone is silent for a while. Finally, Momma huffs out her breath and says, "What's done is done. Can't undo it." Then she is done dealing with the situation and goes to sit in the car.

"You know," says Pop. "She was right worried about you two. We all were. That was a fool thing to do."

"I know, Pop," says Dino. "I should have said no. I didn't think we'd be so long, but that's no excuse."

"No, it's not," says Pop. "We're in a hotel down the street. You two can ride with Destiny and Anderson. I'm not so sure Momma wants to look at the two of you right now."

"Yes, Pop," says Dino.

Pop gets in his truck and drives away. Dino parks the moving truck out of the way and then they get in Destiny's car.

"They'll cool down in a little while," says Destiny.

"I know," says Dino. "I'm sorry, sis. This was your big moving day and all."

"Like Momma said, what's done is done. But we could all use some sleep."

"You said it," says Anderson.

They want to be well-rested so they can move everything into Destiny's apartment first thing in the morning. Destiny sighs as they drive off to the hotel. Tomorrow is another day.

Chapter 10
Epilogue

Dino, Demarcus, Alexander, and Carlos were not thrilled that Destiny's apartment was on the third floor of the apartment building, but they got everything of hers up there the next morning and it only took them an hour. Then they spent an hour helping Destiny get her bed set up and the furniture positioned where she wanted it.

Saying goodbye was hard for Destiny. "Goodbye, Momma," Destiny said through her tears.

"Not goodbye, my child," said Momma. "Just see you later."

"It feels like goodbye," said Destiny, "and this is way harder than saying goodbye to the house."

"I know it," said Momma. "Now you take good care of yourself, ya hear?"

Destiny nodded. Pop put on a brave face as he hugged Destiny and gave her a big kiss. Anderson gave her a big hug before getting into the truck with Momma and Pop. He was squished in the back with Alexander and Carlos, but he didn't seem to mind.

Saying her goodbyes happened hours ago. Now it is late in the day. Destiny is sitting on the sofa in her new apartment, staring at the boxes piled in front of her. She went and got some takeout at a Chinese restaurant down the street, her favorite, sweet and sour chicken balls, fried rice, and ShangHai Noodles. The food was good and now the boxes of food are spread out on her coffee table, her tummy comfortably full.

Destiny spent a good bit of time cleaning the bathroom, hanging the shower curtain, and setting out the bathmats. Everything matched and she loved the look of the bathroom, with the colors of yellow and blue. She also managed to unpack her bathroom items and a lot of her kitchen things. She had to wipe out the cupboards first, just to make sure they were clean enough to suit her standards, but mostly because Momma told her to make sure she did a once-over of the whole apartment.

Now she is done for the day. Sitting in the silence of the late evening, Destiny's mind begins to wander. She had been busy all day, so she didn't have time to think about being on her own. Now, in the silence of her apartment, with strange noises coming from other parts of the building and outside, it is beginning to sink in that she is no longer home.

As she hears a woman laugh outside, homesickness begins to grow in her heart and spread through her chest, making it ache for home. There is a feeling of permanence about this that she always knew was there, but hadn't really let herself feel before now. It was easy to ignore the issue when moving to Texas was still something she was *going* to do.

Now she is here and it's tough. Destiny makes an effort to think about why she moved. Yes, there is her teaching job, which is incredibly important, but there is also a bright future in terms of her tutoring business, something that was limited in how big it could grow back in Louisiana. Austin is so big that even if it takes a while, there is great potential for growing Get Your Mind Right Tutoring far beyond the size it was, allowing her to help more kids than ever before.

Yes, even if she has a hard time adjusting to living away from her family, Destiny knows this move is the very best thing that could have ever happened to her. The key will be to keep busy and make new friends so she will feel a part of the Texan landscape.

As Destiny cleans up after dinner, she is sure she can do it. She will start tomorrow by taking some time from unpacking to explore her new neighborhood. For now, she cleans the few dishes she used and then goes into her bedroom to make up her bed. She is exhausted and hopes she can sleep. She wants to be bright and fresh for her new day and her new life in Austin!

About the Author

Alicia Linelle Holland was born and raised in Many, Louisiana and got her middle name after her mother, Vera Linelle. When Alicia was in middle school, she started the Secret Sister Club that you read about in the Linelle Destiny Book Series. Alicia Holland has been working towards bringing back the Secret Sister Club as she embarks upon quite an interesting life and spiritual journey. At age 26, she earned her Doctorate in Education so that she can be in a position to help others believe in themselves and go far. At age 31, Dr. Alicia Holland opened a Not for Profit, Alise Spiritual Healing & Wellness Center and was officially ordained as a Minister. As a Transformational Life Coach, Professor, Author, Speaker, and Minister, Dr. Holland travels the World sharing her message: "You are Loved, You are Valued, and You are Competent.

Dr. Alicia Holland has two beautiful daughters, ages 7 and 9, who travels the World with her and are active participants in the Secret Sister Club Mentoring Program. She and her family resides in Austin, Texas and are currently looking for a new puppy.

Dr. Holland is available for speaking engagements and can be reached at support@thesecretsistersclub.com or support@iglobaleducation.com.

www.ingramcontent.com/pod-product-compliance
Lightning Source LLC
Chambersburg PA
CBHW071210130626
46555CB00004B/1651